Runaway Wolf

The Bite-Sized Shifters Series

by

Rose Bak

Table of Contents

Copyright

1.　　https://paperorpixels.com/

About This Book

A runaway bride walks into a bar...and finds her fated mate!
Security Chief Duncan has just about given up on finding love. Almost everyone around him has paired up, but he's still a lone wolf. Until a woman in a wedding dress appears in the doorway of his favorite watering hole...

Elizabeth fought her way out of her old-fashioned pack. About to turn forty, she's ready for a new start in the shifter town of Greysden. She's ready to be independent and to finally live life on her own terms. What she's not ready for? An overprotective wolf who claims she's his mate the minute she steps paw in her new town.

It's getting harder and harder to reject Duncan when he's around all the time, being the friend she needs. And when danger from her past comes calling, Elizabeth needs to make a decision: accept her fate or run away.

"Runaway Wolf" is a steamy midlife paranormal romantic comedy with strong women, cinnamon roll shifter men, and a town full of nosy matchmakers determined to help everyone find their happily ever after.

Bite-Sized Shifters", a series of paranormal romantic comedies you can read in just a few hours. Each book in the series is standalone featuring a mature couple, steamy scenes, a lot of fur and claws, and a guaranteed HEA.

Join My Mailing List

Join Rose Bak's mailing list at bit.ly/RoseBakNewsletter[1]. You'll get a free book and be the first to hear about all the latest releases, special sales, free books, and funny stories about my dog.

1. https://d.docs.live.net/ae511949052ccd53/Documents/bit.ly/RoseBakNewsletter

Dedication

This book is dedicated to everyone who goes through hell to make the right decision for them – and finds joy because of it.

Chapter One

Duncan

"Hey Duncan, have you seen my sisters?"

I looked up to see Pepper Rosewater standing by my elbow. I'd been so lost in thought I hadn't even noticed her come up. Some wolf I was. If she'd been a predator she could have ripped my throat out. Fortunately, she was only a witch, and not a very good one at that. I sent the pretty brunette a smile.

"Hey Pepper, no they haven't gotten here yet. I don't know about Cami, but when I left the office Preston was banging your other sister in our conference room. Loudly."

Preston was my boss, and the mate of Pepper's sister Meri.

"Gross. Those two never stop."

She wasn't wrong. My rich shifter boss and his bohemian psychic mate could not be more different, and they liked to bang out those differences. Energetically and often.

"Can I buy you a drink while you wait?" I offered.

"Sure. Thanks."

I waved my hand to Marie, the bartender. Marie was a fellow wolf who was mated to the owner of this establishment, a bear shifter named Ben Murphy. She was a few years younger than me, but like me, she'd grown up here.

"Hey Pepper, what'll it be?" Marie asked.

Marie knew pretty much everyone in town by name. She'd worked at this bar for as long as I could remember.

"I'll take a lemon drop please Marie. And put it on Duncan's tab."

"Coming right up."

I turned to face Pepper, wishing not for the first time that she was my mate. Even though she wasn't a shifter, she was strong and smart and beautiful, the perfect woman for me. On paper at least. Pepper and I had a lot of friends and family in common and spent a lot of time in each other's orbit, but unfortunately she felt more like a little sister to me than anything.

I was starting to despair about finding my mate. At forty-five, I was way past the point I thought I'd be settling down. I didn't care about having cubs, but I did want a companion to grow old with.

Maybe I should do some traveling. It was highly unlikely that my fated mate would randomly show up in the small town of Greysden where we all lived. Then again, I'd lived in New York City for years and had no luck there either. Maybe I was doomed to be a lone wolf.

Marie returned with Pepper's drink.

"How's the witch training going?" Marie asked my companion.

Pepper had grown up in a family of witches and psychics thinking that she was the only one without powers until her cousin had come for a visit last Halloween. It turned out that her aunt had accidentally bound Pepper's magical powers with a spell she'd done on her daughter. The truth had come out when Pepper's cousin Jane came back to the family estate just outside of Greysden looking for answers about her suddenly emerging magic.

Jane had also found a mate while she was in town, a demon wolf hybrid named Gabe who happened to be my long-lost half-brother.

See? Pepper and I had a lot of connections. And now that my friend Dianne and Pepper's sister Cami had found their mates too, Pepper and I were also the only two in our group who weren't mated yet.

"My training is going okay, kind of slow," Pepper answered.

"Well, you didn't have a lifetime to hone your skills," Marie reminded her. "Be patient with yourself."

"That's what my mother tells me too," Pepper acknowledged.

Pepper's mother was a strong witch. Now that her daughter's magical skills had been unleashed, she was trying hard to provide her with all the training she'd missed growing up thinking she was non-magical.

Just then the door to the bar opened, and something made me look up. There, framed in the doorway, was a woman who appeared to be wearing...a wedding dress? I sniffed the air, smelling something sweet. Suddenly my wolf went crazy inside me.

"Mate!" he said excitedly. *"Our mate is here!"*

I popped off my bar stool like the thing was electrified, my wolf pushing me to go to the woman, to grab her and take her back to our den where we could mark her and mate with her.

"What's wrong?" Pepper's voice seemed like it was coming from far away. All of my attention was focused on the mysterious woman who was still standing in the doorway, looking around curiously.

"Mine!" I growled.

"Oh no, not again!" Pepper yelped in exasperation. "Why does this keep happening to me? Am I doomed to be the town's mate magnet who never has a mate of her own?"

Much to her annoyance, Pepper was like a lucky charm for finding a mate. She'd been with every single person in our circle at the exact moment they found their mates. I knew it bugged her, given that she still hadn't found her own mate, but right now I could only focus on one thing: claiming my mate.

I stalked across the room as the woman finally closed the door and headed inside, moving towards the bar.

"Mate! Mine!" I growled.

The woman stopped dead, sniffing the air as her eyes went right to me. She was a curvy beauty with round hips, a narrow waist, and full breasts. I was guessing she was in her late thirties, with pale skin and light brown hair that was up in some kind of complicated twist that accented her sharp cheekbones and pointy chin. My eyes dropped to her mouth, noting her pale pink lips, thick and full.

As I got closer I realized that she was also a wolf shifter. That made things easier. With another shifter I wouldn't have to worry about explaining about mates or wasting time on stupid crap like dating. We could get right to the claiming. Hot damn, this was my lucky day!

My wolf was scratching at my insides, begging to be set free to be closer to his mate.

"Mate!" I said again, stopping in front of her.

The woman's face flashed in fear for a nanosecond before stubbornness took over. She straightened her spine and waved her pointer finger in my direction.

"Oh no you don't, wolf. I'm no one's mate. Now go away."

Chapter Two

Elizabeth

The guy in front of me looked adorably confused. I had to hand it to fate, if I'd wanted a mate, this wolf would be perfect for me. He was tall and broad with wide shoulders, thick biceps, and a toned chest that was clearly visible beneath the form-fitting tee shirt he wore. Faded jeans lovingly hugged his slim hips and thick thighs. He looked like he was in his early forties, based on the tiny lines that bracketed his mouth and the corners of his deep brown eyes, but there wasn't an ounce of fat on this guy. He also smelled delicious, the perfect combination of woodsy and citrus.

"Mate!" My wolf was scratching inside me excitedly. *"We found him! It's good we didn't marry that nasty Marcus!"*

My wolf's feelings on the man that up until about three hours ago I thought I'd marry were well known. It wasn't that I'd disagreed with her. I could barely stand the guy myself. But I'd been manipulated into marrying him. Thankfully, I'd learned the truth and escaped before I went through that sham of a marriage.

As I'd run away from the church I'd made myself a promise: I would never let myself be controlled by a man ever again. Not my father, not my brother, and not some dude in a bar who claimed he was my mate.

"Not claimed, it's true. He is our mate," my wolf whined.

"No!" I told my inner beast firmly. "I fought too hard for my independence to lose it again so quickly."

"You're a wolf," the man said, making me realize that I'd said those words out loud. "You know how this works."

His voice was deep and kind of growly. It did funny things to my insides.

"I don't know what you're talking about," I lied. Resisting my instinct to run away, I stepped around him to grab an open stool at the bar.

A woman about my age came over right away, her eyes curious. "What can I get you?"

"I'll have a shot of bourbon please. And a job application if you have one."

The bartender looked me over.

"Don't you have some place to be?"

I glanced down. I'd almost forgotten that I was wearing a wedding dress. I'd been in such a hurry to leave I hadn't stopped to change my clothes. Or pack.

"It didn't work out," I said mildly. That was the understatement of the year.

"I'm Marie," the woman said, reaching over the bar top to shake my hand. "I'm the manager here, and my mate Ben is the owner. Have you ever been a waitress or bartended before?"

"I've got some experience as a waitress, but not mixing drinks," I admitted.

Marie nodded. "We might could use a waitress," she said. "Let me get you an application."

She looked over my shoulder at the male hovering nearby.

"What's gotten into you, Duncan? Why are you standing there staring at my customer like she's a tasty rabbit?"

"She's his mate," a woman on the other side of the bar called. She seemed as unhappy about it as I was. "Once again, Pepper Rosewater helps the course of true love for Greysden's supernatural community."

I had no idea what she was talking about, so I ignored her too.

"You're Duncan's mate? Tell you what," Marie said to me. "We'll forget about the application. How about you come back tomorrow at eleven a.m., and we'll give you a tryout over lunch? If everything goes okay, we'll do the paperwork then."

I smiled for the first time in what felt like months. "Thanks Marie, you won't be sorry. I'm a hard worker and I learn quick."

She slid my shot of bourbon towards me. "First one's on the house."

"Thanks again," I said, downing it in one long pull. I embraced the feeling of the liquor burning its way down my throat. It felt like a cleansing.

The wolf was still standing next to me staring at me intently. I continued to pretend to ignore him, even while I tracked every breath he took.

"Is there are place in town where I can buy some clothes?" I asked Marie. "I left home in a hurry."

Marie nodded. Her curious gaze shifted back to my wedding dress, but thankfully she didn't ask any questions. In retrospect I should have stopped at my cabin to pick up my stuff on the way here, but I didn't want to take a chance on running into anyone from my pack again.

"Head to the right when you leave here. Two blocks up is a place called Gina's closet. You'll find what you need there. Where are you staying?"

"I was planning to get a hotel room or an Airbnb in town."

"Don't do that. We've got a nice little studio apartment upstairs," Marie said. "It used to be mine, but it's been empty since I moved in with my mate. It comes with an employee discount on the rent."

"I don't want to impose," I said quickly. "You've already been so nice to me."

"Don't worry about it." Marie waved her hand dismissively. "You're Duncan's mate. That makes you family."

"I'm not his mate," I protested.

Marie looked skeptical, but just said, "OK then, I guess you can just stay upstairs until you find another apartment."

Her gaze shot to Duncan, then back to mine.

"If you can hang around for a while, I'll show you the space when it quiets down in here."

"Great. I really appreciate that."

I couldn't believe the other wolf was so trusting and generous. It was a big change from where I'd come from.

"Do you want anything else while you're waiting?"

"Just water please, Marie."

I turned to look over my shoulder as the door opened, letting in a group of people. I breathed a sigh of relief when I didn't recognize anyone. I was free, but I still didn't totally believe it. It might take a while. The guy who thought he was my mate noticed my discomfort, of course. Even without touching each other, he could probably feel the tenuous mate bond forming between us, the same way as I did.

"What's the matter, mate?" he asked, his voice soft and gentle. He moved closer, almost protectively.

"Nothing. I'm fine," I said quickly, shifting away from him.

His expression told me that he clearly didn't believe me, but then he was distracted by the group that had come into the bar.

"Duncan! How you doin' bro?"

A dark-haired man clapped Duncan on the shoulder. Based on their resemblance, he was a relative. I sniffed, confused to get a whiff of demon along with the wolf in the man. That was a weird combination. Two other wolf males were in the group, as well as three females who seemed to be human. Interesting group.

"What's wrong Duncan?" a human girl with bicolored hair asked him. "You look like you saw a ghost."

Suddenly she gasped and gripped her head, her other hand coming to Duncan's arm. Someone growled in warning, and I realized it was me. My wolf was not happy about this woman touching our mate!

The woman's eyes opened again, fixing on me.

"Never mind. I see you already know."

"Know what?" This question came from one of the wolves who was dressed from head to toe in designer duds. He was a fancy pants, my father would say, obviously wealthy.

"Duncan found his mate, Preston," the woman said happily.

My eyes widened. How did the human know about my connection to this other wolf?

"She's a psychic," Duncan told me, reading my thoughts.

The psychic's gaze moved to mine, and she sent me a big, warm smile. "Welcome to the family! I'm Meri Rosewater."

Chapter Three
Duncan

Meri's greeting finally brought me out of my funk. I'd spent the last ten minutes staring at my mate like an idiot while she negotiated a job and housing from Marie. I was in a state of shock. I'd almost given up on finding my mate, and now here she was, appearing almost out of thin air. I would have been ecstatic, except for the way she seemed to be not at all interested in me.

All those times I'd dreamed of finding my mate, never once had those dreams included her rejecting me.

I'd seen how she reacted when my friends had come in the door. She'd been instantly on alert. I could sense her wolf's ears pressed back flat, looking for danger. I wasn't sure what was going on with my mate, but I needed to find out. Whether she liked it or not, she was mine now, and I would protect her.

"Let's start over," I suggested, giving her my most charming smile. "I'm Duncan Fields, Jr. I'm the head of security for Preston Industries."

When she didn't respond, I stuck my hand out. "And you are?"

The woman seemed to take my hand automatically. "I'm Elizabeth."

I wrapped my fingers around her hand, noting how small it was in comparison to mine. She let out a little gasp as our skin touched, no doubt feeling the same pulse of electricity that I was feeling.

"Where are you from, Elizabeth?" I asked, taking the stool next to her, and swiveling to face her directly. I decided not to press on the deliberate omission of her last name.

She hesitated. "Um. Montana."

It was a lie. Shifters were like walking lie detectors. We could always tell by the subtle changes in body language and breathing when someone was lying.

"I can't help but notice that you're wearing a wedding dress," I said conversationally, even as I wondered if there was some guy I was going to have to kill to break his claim on my mate.

She looked down at herself, and then back to me. "Yeah."

"But you're not married?"

"No."

I waited for her to elaborate, but when she didn't, I didn't press her. She looked relieved.

"How'd you end up in Greysden?" I asked.

Another long pause. "I needed a fresh start," she finally answered. "I'd always heard that Greysden was one of the most welcoming towns for all kinds of supernatural creatures, so I thought I'd check it out."

She wasn't wrong. Greysden had been founded by a group of grey wolves, but it was completely open to everyone, human or magical. There were no clans or alphas, instead the town had elected leadership like all the human towns. Over the years, Greysden had become home to all types of shifters, as well as witches, fae, demons, Nephilim, and even a vampire family.

I gave Elizabeth a little overview of Greysden as my wolf whined and scratched inside me, wondering why I wasn't just claiming her. Clearly something traumatic had happened to her – I could see her jump nervously every time the door opened. I was going to need to bide my time and earn her trust. I just wasn't sure the best way I could do that.

Marie gave me an assist as Elizabeth finished up her glass of water.

"Duncan, why don't you escort Elizabeth to Gina's Closet so she can pick up some clothes?"

"Oh, no, I'm sure I'll find it on my own," Elizabeth protested.

"Please, I insist."

She rose to her feet reluctantly, and I walked her out, my hand hovering just behind the small of her back. I felt a tingling on my palm from being so close.

"This way," I gestured.

As we made our way out onto the street I pointed out the various shops like I was a damn tour guide. Usually I was a pretty quiet guy, but with Elizabeth, I found myself babbling to fill the silence.

Gina's Closet was owned by a wolf shifter named Gina who'd grown up here in Greysden. She sold "upcycled fashion", whatever that was, and every woman in town raved about the store.

Gina's employee Kat was at the front of the store when we came in. Kat was a tiger shifter who was mated to one of the wolves from the Grey family, descendants of the town's founders.

"Welcome to Gina's Closet," Kat greeted us. "Oh hi, Duncan. Who's your friend?"

"Kat this is Elizabeth. Elizabeth, Kat. Elizabeth is new to town and looking for some clothes."

Kat's astute eyes took in Elizabeth's outfit. "Runaway bride?" she guessed.

Elizabeth's eyes widened. "How did you know?"

"I know the look. Come on, let's get you out of that thing. I can consign it for you if you want."

"Sounds good."

I hovered at the front of the store while the two women made their way through the various racks of clothing, selecting things for Elizabeth to try on. When Kat's arms were full, the two females headed for the dressing rooms at the back of the store, and I settled in one of the plush chairs situated across from the rooms to wait for them.

"I'll keep looking for more clothes that will fit you," Kat said as she walked out.

I heard the rustling of clothing and my dick hardened against my zipper, knowing that my mate was getting undressed in there. My ardor cooled when I heard Elizabeth gasp. I could feel a flash of pain through our growing mate bond.

"Something is hurting our mate!" my wolf confirmed. *"We must help her!"*

Immediately alert, I jumped up and rushed into the fitting room, pulling back the curtain to see Elizabeth standing there in just panties and a strapless bra, her body twisted to view her back. My eyes followed hers to the mirror, where I could see several large bruises along her back and sides, as well as what looked like fingerprints on her arm, previously hidden by the sleeves of her dress. When she turned towards me, I could see that her abdomen and thighs were bruised too.

I felt a white hot rage I could barely control. My wolf pushed at me, desperate to get out and tear out the throat of whoever had hurt our mate.

"Who did this?" I demanded. My wolf was close to the surface, making my voice deep. My fangs pressed against my gums.

Elizabeth's eyes filled with fear. "No one."

"Who did this?" I asked again. "Who hurt you?"

We were interrupted by Kat returning with a stack of clothing. Her shrewd eyes took in the bruises on my mate, and the look on my face. She patted my arm and slid her body between me and my mate, gently pushing me away.

"Duncan, go outside please."

"But..."

"I need you to watch the front of the store for me," she said firmly. "I'll help Elizabeth. She'll be safe with me."

Kat met my eyes, her gaze pleading with me to comply.

"Trust me." Her voice lowered, and I could see the flash of her tiger in her eyes.

I glanced between her and Elizabeth and drew in a ragged breath. Maybe Elizabeth needed a friend right now more than she needed a protector.

"Fine. I'll be out front if you need me."

Chapter Four

Elizabeth

I let out a ragged breath as Duncan left the fitting room.

"Let's try these on," Kat suggested, handing me some clothes.

She sat on the bench along one side of the fitting room, her expression thoughtful.

"I come from one of the old fashioned streaks back in Montana," she said, her voice conversational. "They didn't value females much, or at all really, other than as breeders. It was like living in the eighteen hundreds or something, with the males in charge of everything and females having no rights at all."

I nodded, letting her know I understood.

"Finally, I decided to leave," she continued. "I wanted a life of my own, and not to be under the thumb of a bunch of backwoods conservative assholes. I took a hard beating as part of my price to leave. It was one of the hardest things I've ever done, but it earned me my freedom. They all assumed that I'd come back with my tail between my legs, but even before my bruises healed, I knew I'd made the right decision."

I stopped midway through pulling on a pair of pants. I glanced down, noting that my thighs looked like my back: one big bruise. I hadn't realized how bad it was until the adrenaline faded.

"I came here to Greysden and found a new life. A career. And my fated mate, a guy who would cut off his own paw before he'd think of hurting me," Kat continued. "Duncan is a good guy, and if I'm not mistaken, he's your mate."

"Yeah," I admitted softly. There was no sense in denying it, whether I wanted it to be true or not.

"But I imagine you're going to need some time to recover from what happened. Growing up in those crazy cult-like packs messes with your mind."

I nodded, relieved that Kat knew what happened without me needing to talk about it. She didn't know the details of course, but she'd surmised at least part of the story. It made me feel less alone and ashamed of where I'd come from.

"My unsolicited advice? Tell Duncan that you need time, that you want to take it slow, but let him in, just a little. Get to know him. You don't have to tell him everything now. Give him some time to earn your trust. But don't shut yourself off from love because of those assholes in your past."

My eyes filled with tears, and I blinked them away.

"The mate bond won't let you push him too far away anyway."

Kat pushed to her feet, picking up the wedding dress from the floor.

"I'll go put this in the back. We'll get it cleaned then put it on sale. Now find some new clothes for the new you. And remember, if you need a friend, my door is always open."

An hour later I was following Marie into the apartment over Murphy's Bar, Duncan walking behind me carrying my bags from Gina's Closet. My old pack had insisted that females dress "modestly" so I'd been over the moon with the idea that I could buy clothes that were stylish and flattering. Not worrying about anyone judging my clothing – or anything else – was incredibly liberating.

At thirty-nine years old, I was finally coming into my own.

"You come on down for dinner when you get hungry," Marie told me. "Dinner is on me tonight. That way you don't have to go grocery shopping until tomorrow."

"Oh, I couldn't impose."

"Please, impose." Marie laughed. "It'll give you a chance to observe the dinner service in action. Think of it as research."

Her eyes turned to Duncan who was standing quietly in the corner like he was my bodyguard or something.

"Bring her for dinner."

"Yes ma'am," he said.

I felt a flash of annoyance that everyone assumed that Duncan and I were a unit already.

"He's our mate," my wolf reminded me sulkily.

Marie left, leaving me and Duncan alone. I knew I should tell him to leave too, but the fact was, being around him felt comforting. He was so strong and quiet and steady.

I puttered around the small studio apartment, checking out the myriad of shelves and built-in cabinets, and putting away my new clothing. I'd worn one of my new outfits out of the store, wide legged pants and a loose tunic that gave my bruises some breathing room. Shifters healed much faster than humans, but it still would take a few days for my physical wounds to heal. The emotional ones would take longer.

Without the buffer of Marie, the atmosphere between us turned awkward. Duncan's presence seemed to fill the room. He remained quiet and watchful, as if waiting for me to make the first move. Finally, I couldn't take it anymore.

"Sit!" I pointed towards the couch pushed against one wall. "We need to talk."

He dropped gracefully onto the center cushion, a flash of disappointment crossing his handsome face as I took the adjacent armchair instead of sitting next to him.

"I don't want a mate," I told him, holding up my hand when he opened his mouth to respond. "I, um, just got out of a bad situation with my old pack, and I broke up with my fiancé at the same time. I'm almost forty years old Duncan, and I've never been on my own for more than a few months. I've never made my own decisions. You seem like a great guy, but I fought like hell for my freedom, and I'm not ready to give it up after less than twenty-four hours. I'm sorry."

My wolf grumbled unhappily inside me, and I shushed her, reminding her who was in control here.

"We're not going to be able to fight the mate bond," Duncan reminded me. "Not for very long. You know how this works as well as I do."

"Well, that's the romantic proposal I've hoped for all my life," I said drily.

He had the good grace to look chagrined. "Do you want me to court you? Date like the humans do? I can do that."

"I want you to be my friend Duncan. That's what I need the most right now. Can you do that for me?"

His eyes met mine and held for a long time, and as crazy as it sounds, I could swear that our souls were communicating. Or maybe it was just our wolves. I could see Duncan's flashing in his eyes.

"Okay. I'll be your friend. For now," he said. "How about going for a run before dinner, friend? It will be good to accelerate your healing so you can sleep tonight."

Chapter Five

Duncan

I led Elizabeth beyond the parking lot for the bar and up the road to where we could access the woods. One of the best things about Greysden was that the town was surrounded by woods, providing not only privacy but also easy access for us to shift and exercise our animals. It was what I missed most about Greysden when I lived in New York. Well that, and being close to family.

There was a trailhead a few blocks away from Murphy's, with a large metal box set up next to a bush for the locals to leave their clothes and other belongings. We didn't worry about theft here in Greysden. It was too easy for the shifters and all the other magical creatures to ferret out dishonesty, and no one wanted to face an angry shifter who'd lost his wallet.

Elizabeth and I were both quiet on the walk, each lost in thought. She wanted to just be friends. There was no way that could last long, not if her wolf was pushing her as much as mine was pushing me. Or maybe my feelings were stronger?

I guess I'd been naive to think that I'd meet my fated mate and everything would go perfectly from the start. God knows my friends had all had their challenges before they got their happily ever afters. In retrospect, there was no reason to believe I would have been any different.

"We can leave our clothes here in the storage box," I told Elizabeth as I started removing my shirt. "We use the honor system here in Greysden."

When she didn't respond I glanced her way. She was staring at my chest, clearly liking what she saw. I couldn't help but flex my pecs. Between my shifter genes and the hard workouts I did to keep in shape for my security job, I knew I looked good.

"You're not going to heal up standing there gawking at me," I told her pointedly.

Her face flushed but she didn't respond. Shifters had supernatural healing but being in our animal forms made everything work faster.

Tossing my pants and shoes in the box, I took a deep breath and brought forth my wolf. The transition took over. In the course of a few seconds, my bones lengthened and re-formed, muscles grew and strengthened, and fur, claws, and fangs emerged. Where my human form had been, a large grey wolf now was in its place. As a wolf, I could hear all the sounds of the forest, and smell all the scents around me even better than when I was in my human shape.

For example, I could scent the distinctive smell of arousal coming from my mate. She stood there wearing just her tunic, bruised legs bare, staring at my new form. I tossed my head, mentally telling her to quit stalling, and then glanced away as she finished undressing. I heard the distinctive popping noises of a shift, and then a smaller red wolf stood next to me, nuzzling my flank.

Elizabeth might want some distance, but clearly her wolf didn't.

I trotted off at an easy pace and she fell into place behind me. I led her through the woods, teaching her the geography of her new home. Periodically we'd detour when one of us scented a rabbit or other prey, chasing them just for fun. We stopped at the creek for a drink, the water clear and icy cold as it washed down from the snow up in the mountains, then we headed back towards where we started.

As we ran I could see Elizabeth's wolf growing more confident. It had seemed a bit submissive when we started, but with every tap of her paws on the soft packed earth of the woods, the wolf seemed to grow bigger and stronger until it was running right alongside me instead of trailing behind. I loved it.

I loved her. I knew she thought it was too soon, but I'd seen instalove work before, and this was it. It wasn't just the mate bond, it was the knowledge that my soul and hers were two pieces of the same puzzle.

Connected forever. My human side felt the connection between us just as much as the wolf side. I just needed to convince my mate it was true.

***

"You don't need to walk me upstairs."

"I insist."

I could practically hear Elizabeth roll her eyes. We'd just finished having a late dinner at Murphy's, both of us starved after our long run. As we polished off cheeseburgers – two for her and three for me – along with a giant basket of fries and salad we talked for almost two hours.

I told Elizabeth about growing up here and Greysden, and then moving to New York to find my purpose. I shared the story about how my boss Preston was turned into a shifter by rogue wolves, and our decision to come back here so he could learn how to be a wolf away from the prying eyes of humans. And I regaled her with the funny stories about my friends one by one finding their mates, from Preston to Dianne to my brother Gabe.

"Poor Pepper," Elizabeth said as I told her about the way Pepper seemed to be around whenever someone found their mates. "Hopefully she'll find the mate she's longing for some day."

"What about you?" I asked. "Did you long for a mate?"

Her eyes turned troubled.

"I lied to you before, Duncan," she began. "I didn't grow up in Montana, I grew up a couple of hours away from here in a pack way up in the mountains. It's a place that has very...old fashioned views about, well, everything. I was raised to believe that your mate is someone who can improve your family's position, nothing else. That fated mates are just a fairy tale."

On impulse, I reached across the table and took her hand, wrapping my fingers around hers. I considered it a victory when she didn't pull away. Electricity hummed between our joined flesh.

"There weren't a lot of jobs up there and I felt...oppressed so I snuck away. Escaped. I moved to Denver for a few months and lived as a full human. Then one day my pack found me. They told me that my mother was ill and manipulated me into returning. When I got there, I realized it wasn't true. They basically held me prisoner for a long time, not allowing me to leave pack lands for years. I was finally given permission to get a job in town to help support the pack, but they kept me on a very short leash."

White hot anger was burning in my veins, spurred on by my wolf demanding that we find those who'd hurt our mate and made them pay.

"Then my father and brother tried to force me into marriage with a man I didn't love. He seemed okay at first. He claimed I was his mate, even though my wolf knew it wasn't true. But I had doubts. My family convinced me that because I'm turning forty soon, this was my last chance, my last chance to find a man. They threatened me, saying if I didn't get married, I was going to spend the rest of my life as a prisoner of the pack. So no, I didn't long for a fated mate, because I knew I could never have one. Not a real one."

"And now?"

Her eyes were determined. "Now I've finally gotten away, and I need some time to find myself again."

Chapter Six

Elizabeth

Duncan squeezed my hand gently, and I could feel the sense of comfort and safety he was sending my way. My wolf was practically purring like a kitten, so happy that he was touching me.

"I'm sorry, that was a lot to unload on you."

Duncan shook his head. "I want to know everything about you. Everything."

Suddenly I yawned, making us both laugh. "Let's get you upstairs. You've had a long day."

He kept a hold on my hand, and I couldn't find it in me to object. We walked out the side door and made our way up to the external staircase to the apartment above the bar. When we got to the door, I turned to look at Duncan nervously.

"Um. Thanks for the run. And dinner."

He held his palm out. "Give me your phone."

"What? Why?" I asked.

"I'm going to text myself, so you have my number. You can call me if you need me, okay?"

I fished my phone out of my pocket, handing it to him. A second later I heard a buzzing from his pocket as he texted himself.

"I'm working during the day tomorrow."

"Me too," I said.

"I'll stop by after work and see how your first day went, okay?"

I gave him a smile. "I'd like that."

He looked like I'd just given him the winning lottery ticket. Before I knew what was happening, he pulled me in for a hug. I stood stiffly in his arms for a full thirty seconds before allowing myself to relax against him. The sensation of being hugged was new to me, no one in my family was a hugger. My arms moved around his waist, my head resting on his shoulder, and I just enjoyed his masculine strength. I could feel my heartbeat slow to match his, and I felt sad when he finally pulled away.

"Be sure to lock the door," he ordered, immediately dispelling my warm feelings for him.

"Yes, Dad," I sassed.

He raised one eyebrow. "Don't make me spank you."

I rolled my eyes. "You wish."

***

The next day I headed down just before eleven to start my training with Marie, wearing a new pair of jeans I'd purchased yesterday and a bright green "Murphy's Bar" tee shirt that Marie had provided. I found my new boss arguing in the kitchen with someone.

"Damn it Ben, quit acting like I'm made of freaking glass!"

"I will if you stop taking unnecessary chances. I've told you a million times, let me carry the kegs, mate."

Ah. This must be Marie's bear shifter husband Ben, the bar owner. I cleared my throat and they both whipped around as if surprised by my presence.

"Good morning," I said, sending them a smile.

"Who are you?" Ben asked.

Marie rolled her eyes. "This is Elizabeth, the new waitress I told you about."

Half under her breath she added, "Stupid man, he never listens."

"I listen," Ben protested. "It's just that you're always telling me shit when I'm falling asleep."

"You're a bear. If I wait for you to be totally awake I'll only be talking to you in the summer."

I suppressed a smile.

"Seriously, he sleeps like twelve hours a day, longer in winter. It's ridiculous," she told me. "Come on, let me show you around."

I spent the next two hours shadowing Marie as she explained the menu, showed me where everything was, and demonstrated the point of sale system. I'd done some waitressing when I lived in Denver for those few months, and it all came back to me. Marie must have thought I was doing okay too, because she let me start taking tables on my own by mid-afternoon.

"For right now, I've got you on the eleven to seven shift," she explained. "That means you'll be working through both lunch and dinner service, which will be good for your tip income."

"I appreciate that."

I'd had to mostly drain my savings to buy my freedom. I'd used my emergency credit card to buy clothes yesterday.

We took a break together around four, having a late lunch. Or an early dinner, depending on how you thought about it. Employees could order anything off the menu on their meal break, so I went with a chicken caesar salad and a side of tater tots. They were both delicious.

As we ate, Marie and I chatted. After spending her adult life as a bartender, my boss was pretty skilled at getting people's stories out of them, and before long, I was telling her the high-level version of my life with the pack, the way my father and brother tried to manipulate me into marriage with a man who I didn't love and wasn't my mate, and the price I'd paid to escape.

"Jeez, that sounds terrible, Elizabeth. I know there are still shifter groups like that – my friend Kat came from a tiger sleuth that was similar – but in this day and age, it seems incredible that these archaic ways still persist. At least you're here now."

Her expression turned sly. "Hopefully you'll find your home here in Greysden, especially now that you've found Duncan."

Deciding to take a chance on being vulnerable I said, "I'm not sure why this is happening now. I'm not in a good space to think about a mate right now."

"Oh I get it. Did you know I met Ben right when I was planning to move away from Greysden?"

"Really?"

"Yeah, for years I'd planned this whole around the world trip and when Murph – that was Ben's dad who was the original owner of this place – when he died I thought, 'well Marie, this is your chance to go out and finally live your dreams'. I was packing my stuff and researching plane tickets when Ben showed up and wrecked it all."

"I heard that," Ben growled from behind the bar.

"Shush Gentle Ben, I'm telling a story here," she called.

I'd already seen that playful bickering was the default for this couple, even while their obvious love for each other shone through clear as day.

Marie's attention shifted back to me.

"Anyway, I thought it was the absolute worst time to find a mate, but everything worked out just as it should. And I've still been able to travel, I just bring my mate with me."

Her hand lifted to stroke the faded mate mark at the juncture of her shoulder, the motion seeming to be unconscious.

"Sometimes fate knows what we need better than we do."

She looked up as a group of women entered the bar, dressed in business attire.

"It's time for happy hour. I'll let you take this table."

Chapter Seven

Duncan

"What's the rush?"

I looked up to see my friend and colleague Dianne standing in the doorway of her office, looking amused.

"You're usually the last one to leave."

"I want to see my mate."

"How's that going?" Dianne asked. "I heard she rejected you."

I ground my teeth in frustration. This damn town was full of nosy gossips.

"She didn't reject me," I corrected. "She just wants to be friends first. You know, get to know each other like the humans do."

Dianne laughed. I looked behind her shoulder to see the hulking frame of Dianne's mate, Elijah. The Nephilim arrived promptly at five o'clock every day to pick her up. Sometimes literally. The giant loved to carry her around like a doll, much to Dianne's annoyance.

"I seem to remember that you two needed some time before you sealed the deal," I reminded her.

Dianne's face tinged pink.

"Fine, I'll stop teasing you. Go find your mate. But we're having lunch tomorrow so you can tell me all about her."

"Deal."

Dianne was Preston's assistant, which was a misnomer because the truth was, she ran this damned place. We'd all be lost without her. That's why our boss had badgered her to move from New York with us when we'd relocated Rutherford Industries headquarters to Greysden. Given that she'd found Elijah – or more precisely he'd found her – it had worked out for the best.

Plus, I think my succubus friend loved this quirky town as much as the rest of us.

When I got to Murphy's the bar was busy with the after-work crowd. It was the first of the month, payday for many in town, and the alcohol was flowing freely. I sniffed the air, immediately locating my mate's sweet scent over by the tables at the back of the bar. She was wearing jeans that fit her like a second skin, her round ass looking mouth-wateringly juicy in the tight denim.

Apparently I wasn't the only one who'd noticed, because as I watched, some guy reached out from the neighboring table and squeezed her ass. I felt a white hot rage course through me, and before the asshole could take his next breath I'd pulled him out of his chair by his throat.

"Don't. Touch. My. Mate." I grit out.

The guy's eyes widened in alarm, his feet scrabbling for purchase on the ground. I sniffed, confirming that he was human. We didn't have a lot of unmated humans in town, so he must be a visitor. The guy held his hands up in surrender.

"Sorry man, sorry," he choked out. "It was an accident."

"You accidentally grabbed my ass?" Elizabeth's annoyed voice came from my left. "Yeah sure."

She patted my shoulder. "Put him down Duncan, I can handle this myself."

"But..."

"Put. Him. Down," she ordered, her tone firm. The fingers on my shoulder dug in painfully, thanks to her extending the tips of her claws.

I released the human's neck and he fell to his feet, gasping for breath. Elizabeth pushed past me and shoved the guy in the chest.

"Mind your manners, asshole. If you touch me again I'm going to put my knee so far up your ball sac you'll be singing soprano for the rest your life."

Her voice was little more than a growl. The man paled, looking between us like he couldn't decide who was more scary. Elizabeth's wolf shone through in her eyes, and her fangs had peeked out from between her lips, making her look even more menacing.

"Now get out of here," she said.

The man turned and practically sprinted out of the bar, his two friends following behind him after stopping at the bar to settle their tab.

"Are you okay?" Marie asked, appearing out of nowhere.

"Yeah, sure," Elizabeth responded. "It's no biggie. Nothing I haven't handled before."

"Why don't you take your fifteen minute break now?" Marie suggested. "I'll watch your tables while you calm down."

"Fine." Elizabeth grabbed my wrist, giving me a tug. "You. Come with me."

My cock pressed against my zipper at her stern tone.

Elizabeth towed me through the hallway by the restrooms and out into the alley. The minute the heavy metal door closed behind us, she rounded on me, her beautiful face angry in the dim light.

"What was that?"

My eyes widened. Elizabeth was scary when she was mad. It was hot as fuck.

Our mate is strong, my wolf said approvingly. *And beautiful too.*

"I was just protecting you."

"And what in that scenario told you I needed you to protect me?" she demanded.

"Um."

I wasn't an idiot. I knew there was only one right answer here.

"I'm sorry."

Her hands slammed onto her round hips. "What are you sorry for, exactly?"

"Protecting you?" I guessed.

She stalked forward.

"I don't need any male making decisions for me, or deciding I need protection," she growled. "I can take care of myself."

"I know, but you don't have to, now that you've got me."

She threw up her hands in exasperation. "For the love of..."

Her words broke off as I grabbed her wrist, using her body weight to spin her around to face me. Still holding onto her wrist, I walked her backwards a couple of steps until her back connected with the brick wall of the bar. I lifted my other hand to cup her cheek. Her pupils dilated at my touch.

"I know you can take care of yourself," I said placatingly. "But that doesn't stop me from wanting to protect you, mate. It's instinct."

I took another step, eliminating the scant inch of space between us. My chest brushed against the tips of her breasts. I scented the sweet smell of her arousal underneath her anger.

"Just like doing *this* is instinct."

I crashed my lips against hers, unable to spend even another minute without knowing what she tasted like. She stood stiffly for a long moment, her lips pressed together, before she finally sighed, softening against me.

My tongue swooped in, exploring her mouth, while every cell in my body calmed for the first time in my life. I didn't need my wolf to tell me that Elizabeth was the woman for me, I could feel it in my soul. Releasing her hand, I cupped both of her cheeks in my palms, pouring all my emotions into the kiss.

I knew she wanted to be friends first. I respected it, I swear I did. But seeing another man touch her had made my wolf go crazy with the need to mark her, to make it clear to everyone that she was mine. I rubbed my body against hers, temporarily marking her with my scent until I could do it permanently.

Suddenly Elizabeth stiffened, sliding her palms between us, and shoving me back. She slipped out from between me and the wall, then rounded back to face me, breathing heavily.

"Damn it! We shouldn't have done that," she gasped.

We stared at each other for a long moment before she flew forward. I wasn't sure if she was going to punch me or kiss me. Fortunately, it was the latter.

This time I was the one pressed against the wall while she gripped my hair and brought my mouth down to hers for a long, bruising kiss, asserting the dominance of her own wolf. I rolled my hard cock against her belly, letting her feel how much I wanted her.

Meanwhile my wolf was egging me on, begging me to fuck her, to claim her, to mark her as mine. I could sense her wolf doing the same. Even though we hadn't officially mated, the bond between us grew stronger with every minute we spent in each other's presence. Her emotions were almost as clear in the back of my brain as my own were.

Finally Elizabeth stepped back, her eyes wide, chest heaving. She took a deep breath, erasing all expression from her face.

"I have to get back to work," she said stiffly. "I'll see you later."

I stood leaning against the brick wall waiting for my hard-on to subside and wondering what the hell had just happened.

Chapter Eight

Elizabeth

Kissing Duncan had been a huge mistake. Before the kiss, I could convince myself that I was unaffected by him, that the whole fated mate thing was a mistake. But after tasting him, feeling his hard length pressed against my stomach, seeing his wolf blazing behind his eyes, I couldn't deny it.

We were mates, whether I wanted that or not. There was no longer a question of 'if' we would be mated, only how long I could hold out.

Stupid fate. Was it too much to ask that I had a few years without answering to some damned man?

The next two weeks passed quickly. I worked at Murphy's through lunch and dinner and while waitressing wasn't my dream job, I had to admit I really liked it there. I'd even picked up extra shifts on the weekends. Marie and Ben were great bosses, and everyone else on the team was as hard working and generous as the owners were. Plus, the tips were good too.

When I wasn't working I spent some time adding personal touches to my little apartment upstairs, arranging furniture, painting walls, and hanging pictures.

I'd never felt happier. Knowing I was finally free, working a job I liked, having my own place, and making new friends was doing wonders for my self-confidence. I could practically feel myself coming out from the shell of someone beaten down by life and emerging as a strong, self-assured she-wolf. I loved it.

But if I was being honest with myself, I had to admit that I was also staying busy to avoid thinking about Duncan.

He'd show up at Murphy's every night, asking to be seated in my section. He'd order dinner and keep an eye on me until my shift ended. Then, against my half-hearted protests, he'd walk me upstairs to my apartment, give me a long hug, and head home.

I had to give him credit. He was trying hard to respect my wishes and just be a friend. Periodically I'd hear him growl when some guy was flirting with me, or I'd see his fangs extend when another male got too close, but unlike that first night, he held himself back and let me take care of things on my own.

By unspoken agreement, there was also no more kissing after that night in the alley. I appreciated Duncan giving me the space I needed, although I knew as well as he did that we were only prolonging the inevitable. The more time I spent with him, the harder it became not to throw him to the floor and have my way with him.

By the time we got to my second Sunday in Greysden, I was mentally and physically exhausted, and horny as hell from being around Duncan every night. Sunday was my day off, and Marie had given me Monday off since I'd worked so many days in a row, so I found myself with two long days to fill.

Kat had invited me to join her and some of her friends for brunch on Sunday morning. I met Gina Grey, the owner of Gina's Closet, our local veterinarian Val Lupino, and Susan Grey, Gina's cousin, who was a caterer. They were all strong, vibrant women, and I liked them immediately.

At least until the conversation turned to mates. Because this was a small town, they'd all heard that Duncan was my mate, and that I wasn't ready to commit to him. One by one they told me the stories of how they met their own mates, and the obstacles they faced.

"Is this some kind of mate intervention?" I finally asked.

"Nah, nothing like that," Gina assured me. "Just showing you how we all learned to balance our careers and lives with having a mate. I know you didn't have many examples of that where you came from."

My eyes flew to Kat, and she held up her hands. "It wasn't me. I didn't break your confidence. Ben heard you tell Marie, then he told the guys, who told us."

"The boys are all huge gossips," Gina confirmed. "Whenever something happens with one of us, the rest of us hear it from them first. They're like a bunch of little old ladies."

I shook my head. "It's possible you all are a little too close."

"They're all good guys, and you got one too," Kat said softly. "They do exist."

Her words were ringing in my head as I walked back to my apartment. Duncan was in the parking lot behind the bar, pacing back and forth. Any doubt I had that he was there for me went away when I saw the look of relief on his face.

"Oh good, you're here," he said. "Where you been?"

"Am I supposed to report my comings and goings to you now?" I snipped, suddenly annoyed.

He held up his hands, palms forward.

"No, of course not. I was just wondering where you were since you weren't working."

I felt the tiniest little sense of happiness that someone cared about my whereabouts, then I shoved it right back down. There was a fine line between concern and control.

"As you can see, I'm fine. Did you want something?"

"Yeah, I wanted to invite you to go for a run with me," he said. "I thought it would be good to let our wolves get some exercise."

I was shaking my head before he'd even finished. Even though my wolf was pushing at me to go for a run, I knew I needed to minimize the amount of time I spent with him. My mind was still reeling from the conversation at brunch, and I needed a little time to process what was happening between me and Duncan.

"Thanks, but I have stuff to do."

He looked disappointed.

"Anything I can help with?" he asked.

I shook my head. "No, thanks."

"Okay then, I guess I'll see you later."

I almost changed my mind as Duncan walked away looking like I'd killed his puppy or something. I stood in the parking lot for a long time, watching the space where he'd been, before I headed upstairs.

The first sign I had that something was wrong was when I realized that the door was unlocked. The second was the arm around my throat.

Chapter Nine

Duncan

I walked down the street, feeling the tiniest bit despondent. I didn't understand how Elizabeth was still resisting the mating fever. It was running through my veins twenty-four seven, the strong impulse to spend time with her, mate her, mark her as mine. My wolf had been crazy all week whenever we weren't close to her. He was so bad that unbeknownst to Elizabeth, we'd been hanging out outside her apartment at night to make sure she was safe, sleeping in our wolf form at the edge of the woods behind Murphy's. Maybe it was a bit stalkerish, but the only way I'd been able to sleep was to be close to her, even if the walls of her apartment separated us.

I stopped dead, gasping as the sensation of fear and pain hit me through our burgeoning mate bond. Was something wrong with Elizabeth?

Go! Our mate is in trouble! My wolf was frantic. *Our mate needs our help right now!*

I turned around and took off back towards Murphy's, running full out. Skidding to a stop in the parking lot, I resisted my wolf's urges to charge up to her apartment, instead taking a few minutes to carefully examine the scene, drawing on my years of security experience.

The apartment door was open a few inches, and I could sense fear, distress, and growing anger coming from my mate. She wasn't alone. At least two other wolves were with her.

Creeping upstairs, I pushed the door open a few more inches, straining to see what was happening inside so I could develop a plan. Some big bruiser of a guy had my mate in a chokehold, one arm around her throat and one around her waist, while an older man stalked back and forth berating her.

"You selfish, useless whore," he growled. "I ought to skin you alive."

When the older man stepped up to my mate and punched her in the stomach, my instincts kicked in. With a growl, I slammed my way into the apartment, my fangs descending, ready to fight.

My entrance distracted both men, and my mate sprung into action. She leaned forward against the guy holding her, then used the leverage of his body to kick her legs up. Her feet hit the older man right in the solar plexus, knocking the breath out of him and sending him sprawling on his ass.

Then she slammed her head backwards, headbutting the guy who held her. The unmistakable sound of a nose breaking filled the room, and he let her go, his hands going to the geyser of blood gushing from his face. Elizabeth fell to the floor, then sprung back to her feet, crouching in a fighting stance.

Our mate is fierce! My wolf sounded impressed, but the man who had been head butted was less impressed.

"Bitch!" he grunted. "You broke my fucking nose."

"Get the fuck out of my apartment," Elizabeth growled, moving swiftly to give the man on the floor a hard kick to the ribs. He howled in pain.

"If any of you bother me again I swear I'll rip out your intestines," Elizabeth threatened. "I'm done with all of you!"

My mate was so powerful in that moment I couldn't breathe. Elizabeth's gaze moved towards mine, as if just realizing I was there.

"Hi honey," I drawled. "I thought you might need some help, but it looks like you're doing just fine on your own."

The look she sent me was grateful.

"Out!" she told the other wolves, pointing at the door. "Both of you. I'd better not see you again. Ever."

The man on the floor pushed to his feet, his arm around his bruised ribs. "Ungrateful bitch," he snarled. "Come on Edwin."

The wolf with the broken nose followed him meekly, although his eyes were shooting daggers at Elizabeth. We watched them leave, standing side by side near the door as they got into a battered truck and drove away.

As soon as they were out of sight, my mate sagged. The fight drained out of her, along with all the color in her face. I caught her before she collapsed, picking her up in my arms and bringing her to the couch. I sat down, settling her on my lap, and she leaned against my chest. I could feel a myriad of emotions moving through her as she gathered her thoughts.

"Do you want to talk about it?" I asked softly.

"That was my father and brother," she finally said. "They've both always been...abusive. In my old pack, men are in charge. It's like they're two hundred years behind the times. A few years after I came back from Denver, the pack was really short on money, so they agreed to let me work in town as long as I continued living on pack lands. In my job I met some other shifters and I learned how dysfunctional my pack really was. I squirreled away money in a secret bank account in case I got a chance to escape again. As long as I gave the pack money, lived on pack land where they could watch me, and joined them for holidays and events, they mostly left me alone."

She took a deep and shuddering breath.

"I met this guy at work one day. Marcus. He was from another pack. Very charming. My wolf never liked him, but at first I let myself fall for his charm. No one had ever been nice to me before, no wolf anyway. I didn't love him, but we got along well enough, and I figured, well, I'm almost forty, this will probably be my only chance to get married, so why not mate with him and join another pack. I figured any other pack had to be better than mine. As I mentioned before, my family was really pushing me to marry him, threatening to take away what little freedom I had if I didn't agree. I guess that should have been a red flag."

She paused for a long moment, lost in her memories, then continued.

"The night before the wedding, I was having serious doubts. My wolf was pushing me hard not to go through with it. There was...an incident with Marcus. I told him I wasn't sure if I wanted to go through with the wedding. He got a little...pushy with me. He slapped me. I was so shocked I told him I wasn't going to marry him."

She was silent for several minutes before I asked gently, "What happened next?"

"I guess Marcus went right to my family and told them that I was calling off the wedding. My brother and a couple of his pack friends grabbed me in the middle of the night, and they beat me up pretty badly. They said I was bringing shame on the family, and on our pack, and I needed to go through with the wedding. I felt like I had no choice, so I got up the next morning and put on my wedding dress. But then I overheard Marcus talking to my father. It turned out that my father had offered me in exchange for a gambling debt that he owed Marcus. He never loved me, never even been attracted to me really, he just saw me as someone he could trot out for events where he needed a mate. And a way to control my father and his pack to do his bidding."

I rubbed her back, willing my wolf to calm down. He wanted to chase down every male who'd hurt our mate and rip their throats out. I remembered seeing how badly bruised she was that day she came into town, and now I knew why.

"I confronted my father and Marcus and things got ugly. Finally I got Marcus to agree to release my family from any obligations if I paid the debt they owed. So I drained most of my savings to pay Marcus and got the hell out of there. Then I just drove south. Something was telling me to come here in Greysden, even though I'd never been here."

"How did your family find you here?" I asked curiously.

"I think there may be a tracker on my car or my phone. Or somehow they traced my credit card? I'm not sure."

"I'll figure it out for you," I promised. "I'll get my team on it right away."

"They were here for more money," she continued. "They said I'd humiliated them, and the pack still needed the cash I used to give them when I worked in town. They wanted me to either start sending money again or come back with them to the pack lands, and when I said no, well, you saw what happened."

"I saw you kick their asses," I said. "You've never looked so hot."

She looked up, her eyes huge in her pale face. "Really?"

I nodded. "Really."

"You're not upset that I didn't need you to rescue me?" she asked curiously.

"I'm just glad to know you can rescue *me* if I need it."

She rolled her eyes. "I can't picture that."

"Well hopefully neither of us will need rescuing in the future," I said. "Do you need help fixing your door? It looks like they broke the lock."

Elizabeth looked up from beneath her eyelashes. "Actually, if it's okay with you, can I stay at your place tonight?"

Our eyes met and held, the air between us turning electric. I could see the intention in her eyes as clear as day, and feel her desire for me through the mate bond, but I wanted to be sure. I didn't want her to have any doubts before we made a commitment. I'd continue to wait if I had to. Elizabeth was worth it.

"I don't know if I can hold back if you're at my house, mate."

She bit her lower lip and took a deep breath.

"I don't want you to hold back. Not anymore."

Chapter Ten

Elizabeth

I packed up a few things then followed Duncan to his truck. We were both quiet on the drive across town. I couldn't believe that my father and brother had come looking for me. Or maybe I could. I'd given them a lot of money over the years while they mostly sat on their asses doing nothing.

Going into my apartment alone after seeing that the door was open had been stupid of me. It let my brother get the jump on me, grabbing me from behind. I should have paid more attention. Should have noticed his scent, and my father's, permeating the air but I'd been so focused on who might have broken in neither of them had crossed my mind. I'd been so comfortable in Greysden that I'd become a bit complacent even in two short weeks.

I was proud of the way I'd defended myself. Honestly, I felt pretty good about causing them some pain, the way they'd done for me. I wasn't normally a violent person but when my father had hit me in the stomach, something had snapped inside me. A lifetime of mistreatment released a swell of righteous anger.

I'd been shocked by Duncan holding back, and by his casual acceptance that I could take care of myself. Many guys, especially alpha wolves, would have jumped in or felt emasculated that I didn't need them to save me. Clearly the conversation we'd had about him going after the guy in the bar who'd grabbed my ass had actually taught him something. It meant a lot that Duncan had let me do what I needed to do, knowing that he would have jumped in if I needed him though.

His confidence in me was empowering. It also smashed through the last of my fears about mating with him. As he'd comforted me on his lap I knew I was done waiting. This wolf was going to be mine. Tonight.

"We're here," Duncan announced.

I looked around, seeing a cute little bungalow on what looked like a quiet street. My wolf was beside herself with happiness that we were going to Duncan's den.

"Do you own this place?" I asked.

"My parents used to live here," he explained. "They downsized into a smaller place and decided to give it to me as an early inheritance."

"Wow, that's nice."

Much better than the punch in the stomach you got from your father, I thought wryly.

I followed Duncan through the door. He held my hand and walked me around, giving me a tour of the two-bedroom house. It was adorable. Clean and comfortable, with large rooms and a huge yard that backed up to the woods like so many houses in Greysden.

"I love it," I told him as we ended up back in the living room where we'd started.

Duncan's eyes shone with pleasure.

We stared at each other almost awkwardly, as if we were both afraid to make the first move. Deciding to be brave, I took a step forward, and then another. Sliding my hands up to his shoulders, I met Duncan's hot gaze. I could see his wolf behind his eyes and knew he could see mine. I lifted to my toes and pressed a quick kiss on his lips. I could practically feel Duncan holding himself back.

"Are you sure, Elizabeth? I know you wanted to wait. Please...be sure."

The truth was, I'd never been so sure about anything in my life. Even though I'd only known Duncan for a little less than two weeks, I knew him at a primal level. I knew instinctively that he'd never hurt me. He'd given me time when I asked him for it, and he'd allowed me to take back my power today. Most importantly, I felt the devotion of his wolf through the mate bond, and knew he felt mine.

I'd planned to be alone for a while before I took a chance on another relationship, but I couldn't run away from this. It was bigger than both of us. Stronger. And it felt more right than anything I'd ever experienced in my life.

"I'm sure," I told him softly.

Before I took my next breath I was upside down, tossed over Duncan's shoulder as he stalked into the bedroom.

"Put me down you idiot," I laughed, smacking his ass with my hand. "You'll strain your back."

"Are you insulting my manhood?" he teased, setting me down in the bedroom. "I'm strong enough for you mate, believe me."

I reached my hand up to cup his rough cheek. "You're kind enough for me," I corrected. "That's way more important to me."

His lips met mine in a rough, claiming kiss. Thick fingers dug into my hair, holding my head in place as he nipped on my lower lip. I opened for him with a sigh and met his questing tongue with mine. My entire body started vibrating with desire as if Duncan was one of those machines, shocking me back to life.

I struggled to unbutton his shirt, then just gave up, using my wolf strength to rip the fabric apart, sending buttons flying. Duncan pulled away with a smile.

"In a rush, love?"

"Yes," I said impatiently. "Get naked."

His smile widened as his fingers went to his belt.

"You're the one who wanted to go slow. Be friends first, like the humans do."

"I was an idiot," I grumbled as I pulled my shirt over my head.

Duncan's eyes widened as I practically ripped my bra off, releasing my full breasts. His eyes traveled over them, his gaze so intense it almost felt like a caress.

"You're still dressed," I reminded him impatiently. "Quit acting like you've never seen boobs before."

"I've never seen yours before," he reminded me, but while he spoke he shoved his pants down, taking his underwear with them, and then it was my turn to stare. Duncan's cock was a work of art, thick and long and erect. I licked my lips, suddenly desperate to get a taste of him.

"Nope," Duncan said firmly. "We can play around later. I need to be inside you, mate. Now."

"Spoilsport," I pouted.

"It's payback for making me wait so long," he rejoined.

"We've known each other for like ten days," I reminded him.

"It feels like ten years that I've been waiting for you," he said fervently. "Now take off your pants."

I shimmied out of my jeans and panties, deliberately teasing him, gratified by the look of fevered desire on his face. This was how it was supposed to be. Marcus had scarcely looked at me during sex. Duncan looked like he wanted to eat me alive. The difference was startling.

My pants were still pooled around my ankles when Duncan picked me up by the waist and tossed me onto the center of the bed. He removed my shoes, then pulled my jeans and panties the rest of the way off. When I was spread out on the bed fully naked, he crawled over me, lowering his torso to give me another long, breathless kiss.

I spread my legs, allowing his hips to settle between them, his cock rubbing against my folds with an eagerness that I shared.

"Duncan, I want you to fuck me now," I gasped when he pulled away, starting to move downwards. As much as I wanted to feel his tongue on my pussy, I wanted his cock more.

"We've got our whole lives for foreplay. Let's get to it."

Chapter Eleven

Duncan

Elizabeth's words were like lighting a match to dry tinder. I growled deep in my throat as I notched my cock against her opening and punched my hips forward, sliding all the way inside her with one long thrust.

She sighed deeply, lifting her legs to wrap around my waist.

"Oh my God, I feel so full." Her voice was thick with pleasure.

I paused, intending to give her some time to adjust, but she tapped her heels against my back. "Move, Duncan, please."

Bracing some of my weight on my elbows on either side of her, I began pounding into Elizabeth like it was the last chance I'd ever have to be inside of her instead of the first.

My wolf was pushing me forward, spurring me on to fuck her so hard and so deep that we'd obliterate the memory of every other man who'd dared to be with our mate. He was in a frenzy now that we were so close to sealing our bond as mates.

She lifted her hips, meeting me thrust for thrust, taking me impossibly deeper.

"Fuck, I'm so close already," she gasped.

I lowered my head, thrusting my tongue into her mouth, mimicking the rhythm of my hips. When we pulled apart, we were both breathless. I saw the glint of Elizabeth's fangs a split second before she lifted her head and bit into my shoulder. Her claiming bite triggered my orgasm, filling me with a sense of peace and power and completeness that I couldn't describe.

Lowering my head, I gripped the meaty part of her shoulder between my own teeth, breaking the skin and sealing the magical bond between us.

Elizabeth howled, her wolf thick in her voice, and then her internal muscles were contracting, her body shaking with the force of her orgasm.

She milked the last of my cum from my body as I licked the wound, sealing it.

Her orgasm seemed to last forever, until she finally sagged to the mattress, and I fell on top of her, sated from my own release. I couldn't stand the idea of separating our bodies, so I turned us to our sides, one of her legs over my hips to keep us connected. We lay there staring into each other's eyes, both of us feeling a sense of wonder as the mate bond strengthened between us.

"Wow." Elizabeth's whispered exclamation was filled with meaning.

"Yeah." My voice sounded like ground glass.

I couldn't believe after all these years of searching for my other half, the mating had finally happened. Elizabeth was perfect for me in every way, just as fate had intended.

We lay still for a few moments, wrapped in each other's arms, before my mate wiggled her hips, eyes widening.

"Are you getting hard again? How is that possible?"

I leaned forward to kiss her. "I can't get enough of you, I guess."

"Wow, you've got some impressive recovery time, mate."

My cock jumped inside her at the term. It was the first time she'd called me that.

"How about you get on your hands and knees, and I'll show you just how fast I can recover?"

I'd been fantasizing about taking her from behind since the moment I saw her. After a moment's consideration, Elizabeth slid back, separating our bodies, making us both groan with the loss.

"Okay we'll do it your way, but next time I get to be on top," she said, her voice firm enough that it made my cock twitch. "I'm not going to be a submissive woman, not in bed and not in life, you should know that right now."

"I already knew that, mate."

I reached over her hip and smacked the closest ass cheek. "Hands and knees."

She rolled her eyes. "I hate bossy," she grumbled as she shifted up into position.

I rubbed my hand over the curves of her fine ass, grateful for the gift of her submission, then slid my fingers through her dripping folds.

"Your body seems to like bossy just fine," I teased.

I kneeled behind her, spearing her with my cock, and we both moaned. Gripping her hips, I started pounding into my mate, taking her rough and hard. She pushed her hips back against me, letting me know that she liked it as much as I did.

It didn't take long before she was shouting her orgasm, her body shaking beneath me so hard that her arms gave out and her upper body sagged to the bed. My fingers pressed harder into her hips, the tips of my claws piercing her skin to mark her again, and I groaned as I painted her internal walls with my release.

When I was finally done, I collapsed on top of her, trapping her between me and the bed for a long moment. I kissed along her shoulders and the back of her neck until she wiggled beneath me.

"Dude, you're squishing me!"

I chuckled, levering off her to lie on my back, then turning her over so she could snuggle into my side. Her head came to my shoulder, and she slung one leg over mine, as if she couldn't bear to be away from me.

I knew the feeling.

Chapter Twelve

Elizabeth

Duncan called off of work on Monday and we spent the entire day fucking each other in new and inventive ways. Sure, we did some talking and inhaled a giant delivery order of pizza and hot wings, but mostly we fucked. By the time I returned to my apartment on Tuesday morning, I was pretty sure I was walking funny.

I took a long hot shower, then headed downstairs for my eleven a.m. shift at Murphy's. The minute I walked in, Marie was in front of me.

"Oh my God! You and Duncan mated!" She pulled me into a hug. "Congratulations."

That was the problem with living in a town full of shifters, you couldn't keep a damned thing secret. It figured that my boss could smell our newly mingled scent.

"I guess you'll be moving out of the apartment?" she said.

"Um, you know, we haven't really talked about it."

Suddenly I felt a little nervous, like everything was moving too fast. My wolf was sure about being with Duncan, but the human part of me, the part where my brain resided, was wondering what I was doing. I'd known the man for less than two weeks. I'd marked him, let him mark me, tying us together forever. Yet what did I really know about this guy?

You know he's perfect for us, my wolf chided. She had no patience for my dithering.

When he'd kissed me goodbye this morning, Duncan had pressed a key to his house into my palm and whispered, "See you tonight, mate."

There had been no question that I'd be coming back to his place, and the more I thought about it, the more panicky I became. Being away from Duncan, I could think more clearly. I remembered the way I'd promised myself that I'd spend some time living independently for a while. Give myself some time to recover from the trauma of what had happened with Marcus and my family. But the first time I'd let Duncan fuck me, I'd folded like a cheap suit. I'd even initiated the mate mark. What was wrong with me?

I was distracted throughout my entire shift. I already knew that Duncan was working late tonight, providing security for a dinner Preston was attending in Denver. He figured he wouldn't be back home until around nine, so when I finished my shift, I headed down to Gina's Closet, taking a chance that I would catch Kat. I needed to talk to someone who would understand what I was going through.

The store was closing as I got there but when I told the girl working at the counter that I was looking for Kat, she waved me towards the back room. I found my new friend there, leaning over a sewing machine, chewing her lip in concentration. I stood quietly in the doorway, not wanting to interrupt, but then her nose twitched as she scented me.

"Hey Elizabeth." She looked up with a smile. "So it's true?"

"What's true?" I asked.

"You and Duncan are officially mated?"

I nodded, and Kat's expression turned to concern.

"What's the matter? You don't look very happy about it."

To my horror, my eyes filled with tears. I never cried. She jumped to her feet.

"Come on, you're coming home with me so we can talk."

"I don't want to impose," I protested. "Stuart..."

"He's out of town on a job, he won't bother us," she promised. Her mate Stuart ran a very successful construction company doing home remodels.

"I didn't realize he traveled for work."

"Usually he doesn't, but his company is helping someone's mate fix up their grandparents home so they can sell it. He took a crew to another part of the state, hoping to knock it out in a week, but the job was a little more complicated than they expected."

"Oh is that the job Gabriel is on?" I asked, referring to Duncan's half-brother. "Duncan was saying that he wanted to introduce us, but he was out of town."

"Yeah."

Kat and I walked to her house about a half a mile away, mostly quiet as we walked. She led me into a warm, open kitchen, then sat me down at the table, returning with a bottle of tequila, a shaker of salt, and some cut up lime.

"This sounded like a tequila conversation," she explained.

We both took a shot of tequila, grimacing as we followed it by sucking on the lime.

"Out with it," Kat said as we put our glasses down.

"You know the kind of pack I came from," I started. "Old school and hierarchical, with lots of violence."

Kat nodded. "Similar to my streak, it sounds like."

"I just...well I promised myself that I'd be independent for a while, you know. That I'd take some time to recover from everything that happened, but then Duncan was around and...I couldn't resist him."

Kat gave me a small smile.

"Being around your mate, it's definitely hard to resist the mating fever. Call it fate or nature or whatever, but it's all-consuming. Every time I was with Stuart before we mated, every single time, it felt like I was swimming against the tide, you know? Everything in me kept being drawn towards him, and when we were apart, it was torture."

"Yeah, I know the feeling."

Kat poured us each another shot of tequila, but neither of us touched it.

"The thing about growing up the way we did is that it's hard to learn to trust. Hard to figure out why someone is being so nice to us. It messes with your head, wondering when the other shoe is going to drop. Wondering if you can trust anyone but yourself. You wonder why you can't resist the person who says they're your mate, no matter how slow your brain tells you to go. You tell yourself the feelings you have must be too good to be true."

"Exactly. But how did you know, Kat? How did you know for sure that what you had with Stuart was real? That you could trust him? How did you not lose yourself in him?"

She tapped her finger against the faded scar near the bottom of her neck.

"You forget that the mate bond is like the best lie detector test ever. When I focused on the bond, I could feel the truth of Stuart's feelings for me. And he could feel my reticence, so we were able to have an open and honest conversation with each other. He was patient, but I also had to learn to trust him, trust my tiger, and myself. But it wasn't all sunshine and rainbows for us. I needed to teach him how to be the mate I needed."

Kat held up her shot, clinking the glass against mine.

"When I learned to trust that fate knew what it was doing, when I opened up my heart and really listened to my tiger, all my doubts about our match fell away. And they will for you too, I promise."

We both downed our shots just as we heard a knock on the door.

"I expect that'll be your mate looking for you."

Chapter Thirteen

Duncan

I could feel it all day. The impression that something was wrong with Elizabeth. Not that she was hurt or in danger – that would have made me rush right back to Greysden. No, it was more of an impression of doubt, or her trying to pull back from our bond. I wasn't sure what had changed since I'd kissed her goodbye this morning, but something had, and I needed to fix it.

I'd been with Preston and Dianne all day, obsessing about what was going on with Elizabeth so much they both were ready to smack me. Given how much time I'd spent listening to them dithering over their own matings, they both owed me. In the end, it was Dianne who gave me the best advice.

"You need to talk to her, listen to her, and focus on your bond," she said. "When she learns to trust you, and trust herself, everything will be fine. But remember, being a mate is a two-way street. You both will need to learn to compromise, and how to be what the other person needs."

When I got back to Greysden, Elizabeth wasn't at my house. I wasn't really surprised by that. I headed to Murphy's, but she had gotten off of work a while ago and wasn't in the upstairs apartment. Standing on the sidewalk in front of the bar, I closed my eyes and tried to reach out to her through the mate bond. Spurred on by my wolf, I walked until I reached a house a short distance from downtown.

Elizabeth's scent hit me as soon as I stepped on the porch. I wasn't sure who lived here, but my mate had definitely been here. I recognized Stuart Grey's mate as soon as she opened the door.

"Hey Kat," I said to the tiger, "Is Elizabeth here?"

She opened the door farther, revealing my mate. I rushed closer, pulling her into my arms.

"Are you okay?" I asked. "I was worried."

She nodded. "Yeah." Turning to Kat she gave her a hug. "Thanks for the helpful talk Kat, I appreciate it."

Grabbing my hand, Elizabeth pulled me towards the door. "Let's go."

I wasn't sure what was going on, but I followed her.

"Let's take a walk," she suggested, heading back towards downtown.

"What's wrong?" I asked when I couldn't take the silence anymore. "Did something happen? Why are you having doubts about us?"

She looked at me in surprise. "How did you know?"

I tapped my shoulder where the mate mark was still healing. "Mate bond."

Her free hand went up to rub her own mark. "That's going to take some getting used to," she said wryly. "It's bad enough I already share a body with one wolf, now I have to share my emotions with another one?"

"And mine are shared with you," I reminded her.

We wandered into the park and sat side by side on the swings, rocking gently in the fading light. Reminding myself to be patient, I waited for Elizabeth to speak.

"I was freaking out a bit today," she finally admitted. "I was feeling...disappointed with myself that I only made it like ten days before becoming dependent on someone else."

I frowned. "How are you dependent? How were you ever dependent? I thought you said that you worked in town most of your life, supporting your pack financially?"

"I did."

"Well then it sounds like they were dependent on you, more than the other way around."

Her eyes widened. "I never thought about it like that."

"I get that they kept you on a short leash, that you felt like you were under their paws, but when the chips came down, you did what was best for you, even if it was scary," I reminded her. "And now that we've sealed the mate bond, we get to be dependent on each other. We're both strong alpha wolves, Elizabeth. That means we can take turns being the strong one."

Elizabeth stood up, coming to stand between my legs, her hands moving to my shoulders as I continued to rock gently on the swing.

"You mean that, don't you?" she asked, searching my eyes.

I nodded, then placed my hand on her mate bite scar. "Can't you feel the truth of my words through our bond?"

She nodded. "I do."

"Good. Is there anything else we need to work out before I take you home and make you come a couple of times?"

"Only a couple?" she teased.

"It's been a long day," I said. "Plus I didn't get a lot of sleep last night."

A slight flush rose up her cheeks as we both remembered exactly why we hadn't gotten a lot of sleep.

"I want to keep working," she said. "And we will both share the household duties. I won't be a housemaid mate."

"I wouldn't want you to do anything you weren't comfortable with," I told her. "Besides, it would be hella boring sitting around the house all day."

"I don't want pups," she added. "I'm turning forty soon, and honestly I'm not even sure if I can get pregnant, but I've never really been interested in having babies anyway."

"That's fine, I'm not a baby person either. Besides, I don't want to be toddling around with a cane at my kid's high school graduation."

She giggled. "You're a wolf. It's highly unlikely you'll be toddling."

"Well I guess there's only one way to find out," I told her.

"What's that?"

"By spending the rest of our lives growing old together."

Chapter Fourteen

Epilogue – Elizabeth

Christmas Eve

"I can't believe it's Christmas Eve already," I said to Duncan as I put on my shoes.

"It's not just Christmas Eve," he told me, "It's the six month anniversary of our mating."

"It is?" I said, thinking back to last summer. "Huh. I guess that sounds about right. Time flies."

For a guy who worked as a bodyguard, Duncan was surprisingly sweet and sentimental. I'd moved in with him right away, to no one's surprise except possibly mine, but living together had been an easy transition. We'd worked together to redecorate his house, making it both of ours instead of just his. We got along well, more compatible than I could have hoped.

True to his word, Duncan continued to treat me like an equal. We made all of our major decisions together and shared the household tasks. I'd continued working at Murphy's and since he got off work earlier than me, Duncan had gotten into the habit of making me dinner every night. It was heavenly.

"Are you ready to go?" I asked.

Duncan and I were spending Christmas Eve with the Rosewaters. We spent a lot of time with that quirky family, what with Duncan's best friend and boss Preston being mated to one Rosewater sister, and his brother Gabe being mated to a Rosewater cousin. For their part, Mr. and Mrs. Rosewater seemed to have adopted the whole lot of us into the chaos that was the Rosewater family.

Tomorrow Gabe, Jane, Duncan, and I would spend the afternoon with Duncan's parents. I was looking forward to having a nice Christmas for the first time in my entire life. I'd spent enough time with both the

Rosewaters and Duncan's family to know that this holiday would *not* involve drinking, insults, or violence. I couldn't wait.

"One thing before we leave," Duncan said from behind me.

"What, honey?"

I turned around, not seeing him at first, then realized he was down on one knee.

"What are you doing on the floor?"

He held out his palm, revealing a shiny ring. "Elizabeth, will you marry me?"

I looked around in confusion, as if there was a hidden camera somewhere.

"We're already mated," I reminded him. "Did you hit your head and get amnesia?"

"Yeah, we're shifter married, but now I want to be human married too."

"Human married?" I laughed.

He nodded. "We made our decision to mate based on fate, and on our wolves. Now I'm asking you to marry me based on your head and your heart."

I dropped to my knees next to him, feeling overcome with emotion. "Wow, that was super sweet."

"I practiced it," he said proudly. "So, what do you say?"

"Yes, I'll marry you, mate."

He slid the ring onto the third finger of my left hand, then pulled me in for a long, deep kiss. When we pulled apart, we were both breathing heavily, and my panties were soaked.

"I love you," Duncan whispered.

"I love you too," I answered. "How long do we have until we have to be at the Rosewaters?"

He glanced at his phone. "About half an hour."

"What would you say if I suggested a quickie?" I asked, looking up at him from beneath my eyelashes.

"I'd say that's the best Christmas present ever."

***

Read more stories from the magical town of Greysden, including Kat's story of escaping her sleuth in "Kat's Dog" and Marie meeting her bear Ben in "Cocktail Wolf". These stories and more are available everywhere at books2read.com/rl/Greysden.[1]

Signup to my newsletter and get a free copy of my contemporary romance "Christmas Angel" by visiting bit.ly/rosebaknewsletter[2].

Keep reading for a special excerpt of "Wolf Doctor[3]" by Rose Bak, part of the Bite-Sized Shifters midlife paranormal romance series.

---

1. https://books2read.com/rl/Greysden

2. https://bit.ly/rosebaknewsletter

3. https://books2read.com/u/4AOXXK

Special Preview

Wolf Doctor: A Paranormal Romantic Comedy

Twilight. Colt's favorite time of the day.

Stripping off his clothes, he took a deep breath, inhaling the scents in the air. He broke into a run and felt his body change mid-stride. In less than thirty seconds he had transformed from man to wolf.

Muscles and bone lengthening as gray hair sprouted all over his body, almost white in some places. His sharp canine teeth extended from his thickening jaw. He felt his tail grow behind him and he wagged it happily from side to side as he increased his pace, moving so fast his paws seemed to barely touch the ground.

Colt's senses were immediately heightened. His vision was sharper, his ears taking in even the softest sound, and his nose twitched with the wonderful scents of the pristine forest.

He headed through the woods, exhilarating in the feeling of free movement. His wolf loved to run. He hadn't shifted in almost a week. Too long. He needed this. He needed to shift and let his wolf run as much as he needed oxygen or food.

Speaking of food, he could use a snack. He scented a group of hares a mile away and headed in that direction at a gallop. His paws ate up the ground as he tracked the smaller beasts, stopping occasionally to sniff the ground and pick up their trail.

There, up ahead, he saw a flash of fur. He moved quickly, ears pinned back, as his wolf took over, the ultimate predator.

He could smell the fear on the hare as it took off, running for its life. Colt pulled his gums back in a canine smile. He loved the chase. The harder the capture, the better it tasted.

He sped up, following the hare instinctively as it took a sharp turn to the side. He pounced, leaping after the hare. Suddenly his feet hit air. And then he was falling. Fast.

Oh crap. He had overshot and gone right over the edge of the bluff. He could practically feel the stupid hare laughing at him as he tumbled down the embankment, scrambling but unable to stop his downward momentum.

He whined as his body hit the road below with a heavy thump.

Before he could recover he heard the squealing of brakes and suddenly he was airborne again. He landed on the asphalt a second time, feeling bones breaking and muscles tearing. He smelled the scent of his own blood and dimly heard voices as he struggled to stay conscious.

"Oh my god Dennis, you hit that poor dog!" The woman sounded upset.

"I'm not sure that it's a dog Sandy, it might be a wolf," someone, presumably Dennis, responded.

Not a dog, his wolf snipped in his head, clearly offended.

Really, that's your top worry right now? he asked his wolf.

Like all shifters, Colt shared space in his mind with his animal. He and his wolf shared not only the same body, but also the same consciousness.

He noted dimly that the humans who had hit him had exited their truck and were watching him cautiously from where they had stopped. He thought about getting up and whined again. The pain was terrible. It was impossible to move.

"He's bleeding and he's in pain," Sandy said, her voice sounding closer. "We have to get him to the animal hospital."

"There's no way he's going to survive," Dennis answered. "Let me get my shotgun out of the truck and I'll put the poor thing out of his misery."

Colt lifted his head in alarm, although it cost him dearly. He made eye contact with the woman, trying to communicate with her. He tried to make himself look sad and unthreatening. He did not want to die on the side of the road, and he definitely did not want to be put down by some random human with a shotgun. With his luck the guy would be a bad shot and make his injuries even worse.

"NO," Sandy said firmly. "You are not shooting him Dennis. Get the tarp. We'll put him in the back and drive him to the vet."

"He's a wounded animal Sandy," Dennis argued. "He may attack us, especially if he is a wolf."

Sandy continued to hold Colt's gaze. "No, he won't," she replied. "Come on, let's get him some help."

Colt passed out, not knowing who would win their argument. He just hoped it was Sandy.

He did not feel the couple cautiously wrapping him in a tarp and dragging him up into the back of their pick-up. He didn't feel himself sliding around in the truck bed as they raced to the animal hospital. He didn't hear the people loading him onto a gurney and wheeling his large body into the hospital. Both his body and his mind were completely shut down now, blissfully blocking the pain.

Then he felt it. A jolt of happiness and peace.

He opened his eyes, staring through the pain as an angel looked down at him. The overhead light glowed behind her like a halo. Thick brown hair framed her beautiful face. Her eyes were deep brown and impossibly kind.

"What happened?" his angel asked. Her voice made him feel calm. She seemed familiar.

"I think he took a header off a cliff. I think he came rolling down from up above. Suddenly there he was, falling onto the road right in front of us," Dennis explained. "Before I could stop, I hit him with my truck. I didn't do it on purpose, he seemed to come out of nowhere."

The angel's hand dropped gently to his head, rubbing him softly between his ears. He closed his eyes again, pressing against the warmth of her hand and whining softly. He had one thought before he passed out again. *Mate!*

***

For more of Colt and Valerie's story, check out "Wolf Doctor" by Rose Bak. Available now for download[1] at all major online retailers. Binge the whole series today.

Other Books by Rose Bak

Magical Midlife Series
Beltane Magic (prequel)
Love Potion
Psychic Flashes
Halloween Surprise
Giant Love
Kitchen Magic
Bite-Sized Shifters Paranormal Romance Series
Long Distance Wolf
Wolf Doctor
Kat's Dog
Designer Wolf
Wolf Sheriff
Cocktail Wolf
Second Chance Wolf
Runaway Wolf
Holidays with the Shifters Series
Santa's Claws
Bear Humbug
Jingle Bear
Silver Paws
Joy to the Wolf
Lion's Heart
Boozy Book Club Series
Beach Reads
Bubbly & Billionaires
Martinis & Mysteries
Bourbon & Bikers
Midlife Madness
Extra Innings

The Marriage Solution
The Good with Numbers Holiday Romance Series
Love Unmasked
The Thanksgiving Scrooge
Maid for Christmas
Countdown to Love
Valentine's Lottery
Christmas Angel
Loving the Holidays Contemporary Romance Series
Dating Santa
New Year's Steve
Independence Dave
Comfort & Joy
Faking It with the Detective
Dropping the Ball
Island Getaway
Midlife Crisis Contemporary Romance Series
Summer Wedding
Roasting with Rob
Christmas Punch
Disaster Planning
The Oliver Boys Band Contemporary Romance Series
Until You Came Along
Rock Star Teacher
Rock Star Writer
Rock Star Neighbor
Rock Star Lawyer
The Diamond Bay Contemporary Romance Series
Brand New Penny
Fresh as a Daisy
Right as Rain
Reunited Series

Together Again

Finding My Baby

King of the Reunion

Finding My Baby

Standalones

Beach Wedding

Jessie's Girl

Factory Reset

Texas Christmas

Canadian Doctor

Non-fiction

What to Do If You Find a Cougar in Your Living Room: Self-Care in an Uncaring World

It's All About Relationships: Reflections on Love, Friendship, and Connection

Catch up with these and other stories coming soon. Join my newsletter for more information[1] or follow my author page on your favorite retailer.

---

1. *https://storyoriginapp.com/giveaways/62ee758e-068f-11eb-904e-c373f6014fe1*

About the Author

Rose Bak has been obsessed with books since she got her first library card at age five. She is a passionate reader with an e-reader bursting with thousands of beloved books.

Although Rose enjoys writing both fiction and nonfiction, romance novels have always been her favorite guilty pleasure, both as a reader and an author. Rose's contemporary romance books focus on strong female characters over thirty-five and the alpha males who love them. Expect a lot of steam, a little bit of snark, and a guaranteed happily ever after.

Rose lives in the Pacific Northwest with her family, and special needs dogs. In addition to writing, she also teaches accessible yoga and loves music. Sadly, she has absolutely no musical talent, so she mostly sings in the shower.

Please sign up for the Rose Bak Romance newsletter[1] to get a free book and keep up to date on all the latest news. You can also follow Rose on Facebook[2], Instagram[3], Twitter[4], Goodreads[5], or Bookbub[6].

---

1. https://storyoriginapp.com/giveaways/62ee758e-068f-11eb-904e-c373f6014fe1
2. https://www.facebook.com/AuthorRoseBak
3. https://www.instagram.com/authorrosebak/
4. https://twitter.com/AuthorRoseBak
5. https://www.goodreads.com/authorrosebak
6. https://www.bookbub.com/authors/rose-bak

Don't miss out!

Visit the website below and you can sign up to receive emails whenever Rose Bak publishes a new book. There's no charge and no obligation.

https://books2read.com/r/B-A-VATM-TZUOC

BOOKS 2 READ

Connecting independent readers to independent writers.

Did you love *Runaway Wolf*? Then you should read *Santa's Claws*[7] by Rose Bak!

[8]

This year Santa is getting a Christmas present...a brand new mate!Tony is transitioning back to civilian life after twenty years in the military and trying to figure out his next steps. When his mom signs him up to play Santa at Greysden's annual holiday festival, he's not happy about it. After so many years away from his family, he's lost his love of the holiday, and the last thing the grumpy wolf wants to do is spread Christmas cheer.Marissa just moved to town, looking for a fresh start to heal her broken heart. When a growly Santa tracks her down and says he's her fated mate, she wonders if he's got some kind of brain injury. Humans don't turn into wolves, right?Even crazier...falling in love with someone she just met. But is it real? Or just a Christmas romance?

---

7. https://books2read.com/u/bPQrXR

8. https://books2read.com/u/bPQrXR

__About the "Shifters for the Holidays" series:__ The shifter town of Greysden is gearing up for the holidays and some of its sexiest residents are finally finding their true mates. The road to love isn't easy, but with a little help from fate and some nosy small-town matchmakers, there's a guaranteed happily ever after. If you love short and steamy standalone romances with curvy women and growly shifter men who fall fast and hard, this is the holiday series for you.

Get your copy of this instalove Christmas romance today!
Read more at https://rosebakenterprises.com/.